The last bell rang. The teacher walked over to close the door of the classroom—and froze.

A familiar figure shot past her and spun once around the desk. She paused at the corner, and her gaze swept the room.

For one moment, Dr. Morthouse's steely gray eyes met Maria's dark brown ones. Then, suit and all, the principal pushed off and out of the room.

"Outta my way," she shouted at the teacher as she elbowed through the door. "I'm trying to think!"

Then she was gone in a whir of wheels down the hall.

The homeroom teacher staggered back and collapsed in her chair.

No one moved. No one spoke.

It was all too horrible to be true.

But it was true.

It was Dr. Morthouse. And she was wearing Maria's blades.

Other Skylark Books you won't want to miss!

GRAVEYARD SCHOOL

April Ghouls' Day

Tom B. Stone

A SKYLARK BOOK

New York Toronto London Sydney Auckland

RL 3.6,008–012

APRIL GHOULS' DAY

A Skylark Book/March 1996

ISBN 0-553-48487-7

Published simultaneously in the United States and Canada

Bantam Books are published by Bantam Books, a division of Bantam Doubleday Dell Publishing Group, Inc. Its trademark, consisting of the words "Bantam Books" and the portrayal of a rooster, is registered in the U.S. Patent and Trademark Office and in other countries. Marca Registrada. Bantam Books, 1540 Broadway, New York, New York 10036.

PRINTED IN THE UNITED STATES OF AMERICA

OPM   0 9 8 7 6 5 4 3 2 1

GRAVEYARD SCHOOL

April Ghouls' Day

CHAPTER
1

"Excellent !" said Vickie Wheilson.

"Decent," agreed Stacey Carter.

Maria Medina grinned. She was holding a pair of new in-line skates. "I saved up forever to buy them."

"Dumb," Polly Hannah said.

Vickie, Stacey, and Maria turned and gaped at Polly.

Smugly, Polly smoothed her curly blond hair into place. She adjusted the baby-blue headband that matched the baby-blue tights she was wearing. The tights, of course, matched her pink-and-blue-flowered Laura Ashley dress.

Polly's outfit matched, but she clashed with the three girls around her. Stacey wore a green turtleneck and a red windbreaker. Her dark hair was pulled back in a single braid. Maria was wearing one of her huge collection of rugby shirts and a jean jacket. Her bangs, as usual, were sticking straight up and her chin-length black hair was pushed behind her ears. Vickie had on an orange sweat-

1

shirt that didn't match her spiky red hair or her favorite pink high-tops. Her jeans were ripped and her wrist-guards, which she wore for skateboarding and almost everything else, were badly scuffed. All three girls pre-ferred jeans to dresses and tights.

"Dumb," Polly repeated. "Plus, you'll be killed, Maria."

"She will not!" said Vickie. "Blades aren't any harder to use than boards." She tapped the skateboard resting under her left foot with the toe of her sneaker.

Rolling her eyes in disgust, Maria said, "I'm not the one who's about to get killed around here, Polly. Can't you ever say anything nice?"

"Nice?" said Polly, as if the word were a problem on a spelling test. She gave Maria a suspicious look.

"C'mon, let's go," said Vickie, gesturing toward the hill behind the school. The last class of the day at Grove Hill Elementary School, more commonly known to the students as Graveyard School, had just ended. On foot, by bicycle, by car, and by bus, kids were making quick exits from their less-than-beloved school. Except for Sta-cey, Vickie, and Maria, who had plans. Polly, annoyingly enough, tagged along because her mother hadn't arrived to pick her up yet.

"It's not even your birthday," Polly whined on. "Or Christmas or Hanukkah or *anything*. Why should you get new in-line skates?"

"It's April Fools' Day," Stacey joked.

"Not till tomorrow!"

"Are we going to practice, or what?" demanded Vickie impatiently, gesturing once more toward the hill.

A sudden, chill gust of wind swirled down on them, silencing them all for a minute.

Then Polly said triumphantly, "*And* it's not safe up there. I'll bet you'll all fall into an empty grave or something! And die. And never be found!"

Strange things *had* happened up on Skateboard Hill, high above the old graveyard behind Grove Hill Elementary that had inspired the school's nickname. Vickie knew. She'd been there. But she wasn't about to talk about it, then or ever.

Stacey snorted. She'd seen her share of bizarre things around the school. "It's not safe down here, either, Polly. This school can be hazardous to your health."

Maria said, "Are you afraid of *ghosts,* Polly?"

"No!"

"No one ever gets buried up on the graveyard now," Maria went on conversationally. "All the ghosts are probably old and tired. I wouldn't worry if I were you."

"I'm not afraid of ghosts. There's no such thing as a ghost!"

Then suddenly, almost magically, a horn loud enough to wake the dead sounded at the bottom of the school's front stairs.

"I'll say it now, *before* you go up that hill," said Polly, glaring at Maria. "*I told you so!*" She flounced down the stairs and into an enormous baby-blue Cadillac.

The car roared away.

"Finally! I thought we'd never get rid of her," said Maria.

"Forget Polly. Let's get up to Skateboard Hill," said Vickie.

The three girls started to walk quickly up the narrow, surprisingly smooth road that snaked through the graveyard itself, twisting into a bend known locally as Dead Man's Curve. They didn't linger on the bridge that arched over a deep, narrow creekbed carved out by icy water. They didn't even slow down until they had passed between the scarred boulders on either side of the entrance to the graveyard, where the road split off from Skateboard Hill above it.

"Skate!" Vickie waved enthusiastically as her cousin, Skate McGraw, shot past them and disappeared from sight down Skateboard Hill. Like Vickie, Skate had no love for the old graveyard. And he knew all too well the dangers of Dead Man's Curve. But he loved to board, and it was the best skateboard hill around.

Stacey and Maria sat down to put on their blades and their protective gear. Vickie gave her skateboard a routine inspection and put on a helmet and elbow and knee guards.

"Cool in-lines," said Skate as he trudged back up the hill and dropped his board at the top.

He took off before Maria could answer.

"They are nice, aren't they," she said, getting to her feet and sticking one foot out to admire them again.

"They are *beautiful*," said Stacey.

Vickie said, "If I didn't board, I'd definitely want a pair of skates like yours."

With a satisfied smile, Maria said, "I bet my blades can beat your board."

"I can beat you both," declared Stacey.

"No way!" shouted Vickie, forgetting that a contest on Skateboard Hill was the way the trouble had started last time.

The three of them took off.

They skated and boarded until the sun looked like the edge of a red-rimmed eye, glaring at them over the clouds. Then Maria, Stacey, Vickie, and Skate walked down Skateboard Hill, between the rocks and along the narrow road that led through the graveyard to the bottom of the hill.

They walked quickly. And, perhaps because it was getting late and the cold wind that plucked eternally at the graveyard seemed also to be running skeletally cold fingers over their spines, they talked loudly.

"We should tell Polly we saw a ghost up here," said Maria.

Skate, who seldom spoke, said, "No."

Vickie said, "What would a ghost be doing out before dark? Especially since it's not even Halloween."

A gust of wind gave a sudden shriek around a tombstone, and the four of them instinctively drew closer together. Maria felt as if something had given her rugby shirt a sudden tug. She looked over her shoulder.

5

The long shadows of the tombstones seemed to be reaching out toward them like ghostly fingers.

Quickly Maria said, "You're right. Polly would be insulted if a ghost showed up on a day that wasn't an official haunting day. She'd probably try to report it to the principal or something."

Skate gave a snort of amusement.

"Well, maybe April Fools' Day is a ghost holiday or something," said Stacey. "I mean, if I was a ghost, I'd want more than just Halloween for partying."

Was that another tug Maria had felt on her shirt? She looked swiftly around. Darker. Later. More shadows.

But nothing behind them. She was just imagining things.

"Nah, Polly wouldn't buy that," Vickie was saying. "She'd report the ghost to the principal and Dr. Morthouse would probably hunt that ghost down and make it, make it . . ."

"Wish it were dead? Sorry it had ever been born?" Maria joked.

"Well, she's the only person I know who could probably haunt a ghost," said Stacey. She added thoughtfully, "Except maybe Basement Bart."

They all looked in the same direction at once—toward the basement door that was at one side of the school's back steps. The door to the kingdom of the janitor, Mr. Bartholomew.

Had anyone ever gone down there and lived? Or were

the bones of students from past generations crumbling in the dark depths below the school?

Was Basement Bart the ultimate cleaning man?

"I think Polly likes Dr. Morthouse," said Vickie.

"She would," said Maria in disgust. "That only lowers my opinion of them both."

"I didn't think that was possible," Stacey said.

But Maria's mind had gone off in a different direction. "Imagine being the role model for someone like perfect Polly Hannah. How depressing."

"Twisted," muttered Skate.

"Or weirder," Maria went on, "imagine what it is like *being* Dr. Morthouse."

"Euwwwww," said Vickie and Stacey simultaneously, and Skate made what might have been a gagging noise in his throat.

"Seriously. It wouldn't be so bad. I mean, think of all the power," Maria went on.

"Power corrupts and absolute power corrupts absolutely," said Stacey.

"Puh-lease," said Maria. "Like that means anything."

"It means Dr. Morthouse is all-powerful and all-evil," said Vickie cheerfully. "Is that what you want?"

They'd reached the foot of the hill.

Maria said, "I don't know. I just think it would be kind of cool. I mean, haven't you ever wanted to switch places with someone, just to see what it would be like?"

"Like Polly Hannah!" shrieked Stacey.

"Or Basement Bart!" shouted Vickie.

"Jaws," suggested Skate.

They all began to howl with laughter. They walked out of the old graveyard and onto the school grounds just as the last red glint of the sun disappeared from the sky.

They were laughing so loudly that they didn't even notice that last, arctic curl of wind that swept down from the graveyard and wrapped them all, for just a millisecond, in an icy cloak.

But Skate suddenly squinted back up over his shoulder as if he expected to see something bad high up on the hill behind them.

And for that moment, something seemed to cloud Maria's vision, as if the world had tilted slightly.

She shivered and walked hastily out of the graveyard and away from Graveyard School, as if something loathsome were trying to follow her home.

CHAPTER

2

Bentley Jeste, Algernon Green, and Parker Addams walked up the steps to the school. They passed among the first-, second-, third-, fourth-, and fifth-graders, all huddled on the steps in ascending order, without noticing them.

They'd been there, done that. Now they were sixth-graders—top-of-the-stairs members of the Graveyard School student body. Sixth-graders ruled.

Besides, from the throwing gesture that Algie made, and the way Park frowned and thumped his right fist into his left palm, it was clear they were talking about Park's favorite subject: baseball. That meant Park wouldn't have noticed a dinosaur standing by the school's front door.

Well, maybe not.

But just as the three boys reached the top steps near where Maria and Stacey were standing, Algie suddenly stumbled.

He swung both arms wildly. Then he fell backward over the edge of the stone railing with a strangled cry.

"Oh no!" gasped Maria. She and Stacey and half the school rushed forward to peer over the edge.

Algie was lying sprawled on the ground below. The spindly arms of broken shrubbery splayed out under him.

"Algie! Algie!" shouted Bent. "Are you okay?"

"Looks like the bushes might have helped break his fall," said Park.

Algie sat up. He rubbed his head. "W-What happened?" he asked.

He stared up at the row of faces peering down at him.

"Hey, Algernut. You okay?" asked Park.

Algie grinned sheepishly. "Yeah."

Park turned. "He's okay," he announced to the crowd behind him. He gave the lower-graders a stern warning glare. "What's everybody looking at?"

The students began to melt back. Order and hierarchy began to reassert themselves on the front steps. In a moment the front bell would ring and—

A horrible, bloodcurdling scream froze everybody in their tracks.

"Aaaaaarrrrrrowwwwwwww! Nooooo! Oooooooo-ooooh nooooo!"

Algie staggered around the edge of the railing at the bottom of the stairs. He was tearing at his T-shirt, his hair, his face. Black specks flew in the air. The first-graders parted and Algie screamed, "Help me!"

In a single leap, Park had reached Algie. Bentley was close behind.

"*Help me!*" screamed Algie.

Suddenly Bent jumped back, slapping at his own face and hair and clothes.

"Ants!" screamed a little kid, beginning to do a fear-of-ants dance of his own on the bottom steps.

Other little kids began to scream and run.

"*Help!*" screamed Algie again.

"*Owww!*" shouted Park.

"Fire ants! Killer ants!" Bentley gasped. "They're eating him alive!"

Maria watched in horror as the black, crawling specks danced over Algie, flew into the air, fell to the steps. Some of the kids began to stomp on the fallen ants as most of the other students frantically tried to get out of the way.

A spray of ants hit Maria in the face. She ducked, slapping at them instinctively. Something went down her rugby shirt.

She stuck her hand in after it and heard someone begin to laugh.

"April Fools'!" shouted Algie, straightening up. He and Park and Bent slapped each other's hands in victory.

"Someone should report them to the principal!" said Polly angrily.

Stacey and Maria exchanged glances. Maria hoisted

her backpack onto her shoulder. It bulged uncomfortably against her, but that was okay. The bulges were her new blades. She and Stacey and Vickie were going to go blading again today after school.

"Be my guest, Polly. But it *is* April Fools' Day," said Maria.

"Big deal. So what! It's not like it's a real holiday or anything."

"True," said Stacey thoughtfully. "I mean, it is kind of bogus. I think they should give us the day off, don't you?"

"Yeah," said Maria. She turned and pushed open the door of the school. "In your dreams."

"You're not going inside, are you?" asked Stacey in shock. "The bell hasn't even rung yet!"

"I want to put my blades and stuff away," said Maria.

Polly sniffed scornfully. Then she said unexpectedly, "I'll go with you. I like to get to class early. Maybe I can help the teacher."

She pushed past Maria and walked into the school without waiting for her.

"Teacher's pet," muttered Stacey.

"Teacher's pest," said Maria. "Wouldn't you hate to be a teacher and have *that* coming to class early?"

"Yesterday you wanted to be a principal," said Stacey. "Dr. Morthouse, remember?"

"That's different," said Maria. She smiled as pushed her way into the school. Over her shoulder she added, "If I was Dr. Morthouse, I could have Polly *exterminated*. Like the pest she is."

* * *

"Boo!"

Maria jumped and gave a stifled scream in spite of herself. Then she spun around. "Ha, ha, you're dead, Vickie."

Vickie grinned. "What're you doing at school so early?" She lowered her voice and looked around. "Aren't you afraid of lurking principals?"

"No," said Maria. She finished unloading her blades into her locker. She was about to close it when Vickie said, "Wait."

"Why?"

"I just had a phenom rocket scientist idea!"

Maria sighed. "Save it for class, Vickie."

"No, really!" Vickie pointed down the hall. "Do you see what I see?"

Maria stared. All she saw was empty hallway, grim gray lockers, scuffed paint, and Basement-Bart-polished tile floors.

"No," she said.

"Board country," said Vickie. "Bladeland. Wheel-o-rama."

"What are you talking about?"

Vickie's eyes were sparkling with excitement. Her spiky red hair seemed about to go off like fireworks. "These halls are perfect for boarding. Or blading. I've always wanted to try it, but it's no fun by yourself."

"Get Skate to—"

But Vickie was shaking her head. "Nope. Won't do it.

He's afraid he'll get caught and his board'll get confiscated." She grinned. "Can you see that? Dr. Morthouse on a board?"

The thought was funny. Also disgusting. Maria said, "What makes you think we won't get caught?"

"The school's empty. We've got at least ten minutes till the first bell. You know the principal is lurking near the front door, keeping an eye on things. You *know* Mr. Lucre is somewhere nearby, trying to butter her up."

Vickie was referring to the assistant principal, a round man fond of brown suits who combed his thinning hair across the top of his balding head. Mr. Lucre had a nervous laugh and was fond of saying things like "Remember, boys and girls, the princi*pal* is your pal."

Maria considered Vickie's words. Wherever Dr. Morthouse was, Mr. Lucre wasn't far behind. "True."

"So let's do it! I have the perfect spot picked out, upstairs back corner. Above the new boys' bathroom."

Maria stared down the halls, seeing them in a new light now. Easy to imagine how quietly, how swiftly the wheels of a skateboard—or a pair of skates—would glide down those halls. No bumps. No rocks or sticks or holes or sand.

You'd fly low, thought Maria. She could almost hear her new blades calling to her from her locker. What had come over her? She was swamped with temptation. Even though she knew if she was caught she'd lose her new blades—probably with her feet still inside.

"C'mon, let's give it a try," urged Vickie.

14

Maria could hear the new blades spinning their wheels, all alone in her locker. She had a sudden vision of flight, of shooting past the lockers in a smooth whirring blur.

"Okay," Maria heard herself say. "Okay. Let's put a wheel on the school."

The hall was vast, gleaming, and empty. The battered lockers stood at attention on either side. The classroom doors were all shut, the classrooms all empty.

Sitting on the steps, Maria tightened her blades and stood up. She checked her gear.

She glanced over at Vickie, who was strapping on her helmet, and gave her two thumbs up.

Vickie jerked her own thumb up and pumped her skateboard forward to line it up next to Maria.

"Let's go!" she said softly.

They took off.

It was like skating on perfect ice. Like taking off in an airplane. Like the plunge from the diving tower at Slime Lake.

The lockers went by faster and faster until they became a blur. The girls' wheels whirred slickly.

In no time at all they'd reached the end of the hall. Vickie stomped on the tail of her board and ground to a halt. Maria, with a little less skill, braked her skates. She still had to grab a locker to make herself stop.

"Whoa," said Vickie. "I thought you were going to shoot the stairs."

15

"Not me," said Maria. She turned and took off back down the hall, with Vickie right behind her.

They went back and forth for as long as they dared, doing weaves, banging on lockers, executing last-minute stops and glass-slick turns. The smooth tile halls hardly grabbed the wheels at all. *It would be easy to lose control,* thought Maria. Good thing there were plenty of lockers and water fountains and doorknobs to grab on to, just in case.

Somewhere far off, a bell rang.

"Morning warning," panted Vickie. "The day is about to begin." She reached up to unbuckle her helmet.

"Just one more," said Maria, dizzy with the thrill of it all.

"Dangerous," said Vickie. "Possibly fatal."

"Chicken," said Maria. She took off again.

She heard Vickie kick off behind her.

Now Maria was moving faster than she'd ever moved in her life. Her wheels felt as if they weren't even touching the floor. The end of the hall, where it turned the corner, came up far too soon.

Far too fast.

Why didn't she stop then? Maria didn't know. She didn't know what made her lean and crouch and somehow make the impossible turn so that she was facing a new stretch of hall.

Behind her she heard Vickie grind to a halt. Heard her call, "Maria? Maria, *don't!*"

Maria didn't listen. She didn't care. She just wanted to

keep going. Faster and faster and faster. Completely out of control and loving it.

Nothing could stop her now.

But she was wrong.

Wicked wrong. Something could.

Something tall. Suit-clad. Iron-eyed and thin-lipped. Something that was smiling a silver-fanged smile as it stepped out into the hall.

It was Dr. Morthouse.

CHAPTER
3

"Moooooove!" screamed Maria.

Dr. Morthouse moved. She crouched down. Her industrial-strength hands reached out for Maria.

In your dreams, thought Maria. *You'll never take me alive.*

She veered left. Facing her, Dr. Morthouse leaned right. Almost completely out of control, Maria tried to fake right, then go left.

Like a killer soccer player, like a dancing partner from her worst nightmare, like an attack image in her mirror, Dr. Morthouse did everything Maria did.

Maria was doomed. Dead.

She hoped they'd bury her with her new blades on.

Just as Dr. Morthouse crouched low, Maria straightened up. She'd meet her fate like a hero. She flew forward. She tried not to scream with terror as Dr. Morthouse's blazing eyes met hers.

Maria Medina hit Dr. Morthouse at top speed. The

crash shook pictures off walls in the classrooms, forced open locker doors. The whole building seemed to shudder.

In the new downstairs boys' bathroom, a geyser of water shot up into the air from the toilet on the end.

In the basement, Bart straightened up. He cocked his head. Then he smiled a terrible smile.

Coming out of the school office on the first floor, assistant principal Hannibal Lucre jumped and clutched at his heart. "Oh dear, oh dear," he muttered, looking wildly around.

At the far end of the hall, Vickie peered cautiously around the corner.

The hall was quiet. Deathly still.

Hastily tucking her skateboard out of sight so that no wandering authority figure could confiscate it, Vickie dashed down the hall toward the wreck.

What she found was shocking. Gruesome. Painful to see.

Dr. Morthouse, the principal of Graveyard School, and Maria Medina, sixth-grader, lay skull to skull on the tile floor. Maria's helmet was askew. Dr. Morthouse's severe French twist had been mashed.

Both of them had their eyes closed.

Vickie squatted down. No blood.

Maria made a funny noise.

Good. At least Maria was breathing. Vickie reached out and touched her arm. If she could wake Maria up, get her away before Dr. Morthouse regained consciousness, Maria might still escape being Morthoused alive in the principal's office—before being suspended for life.

"Maria?" whispered Vickie. "Are you okay?"

Dr. Morthouse said, "Uhhhh?"

Suddenly Vickie remembered that you weren't supposed to move accident victims, in case they'd broken their necks. She hesitated. Maybe she should go for help. Call 911. Shout "Help!"

Maria opened her eyes. She stared blankly up at Vickie. "W-What . . . ?"

"You bladed into Dr. Morthouse. You took her *out*." Vickie glanced quickly over at the fallen principal. "And she took you out, too."

A voice echoed up the stairs. "Oh dear, oh dear, oh dear."

Forgetting caution, Vickie grabbed Maria's arm. "Quick! That's Lucre! We've got to get out of here!"

The urgency in Vickie's voice seemed to shake Maria. "Is there an emergency?" she asked, sitting up.

"There will be, if we don't disappear. Like now!" Vickie hauled Maria to her feet.

The skates almost went out from under Maria. She and Vickie careened crazily across the hall, then caromed off the lockers.

"Whoa, whoa!" gasped Vickie. "Shake it off, Maria. You can handle the blades."

As if to refute this, one of Maria's feet shot out from under her. The other went backward and she executed a painful-looking split.

Vickie and Maria both went down.

Heavy breathing came from the stairwell. Mr. Lucre had paused to catch his breath.

Hardly knowing what she did, Vickie yanked the skates from Maria's feet. She pulled Maria upright.

Maria staggered.

"Oh dear, oh dear," said Mr. Lucre's voice, much too near.

"Run!" whispered Vickie, forgetting about the skates, forgetting about everything except her fear for her life. She clamped her hand on Maria's arm and sprinted forward.

Maria skidded and shuffled and lurched after her, still unsteady on her feet, almost as if she were trying to slow Vickie down.

But somehow they made it. They skidded around the corner and out of sight at the far end of the hall just as Mr. Lucre's head appeared at the top of the stairs.

A moment later, still clutching Maria's arm, her heart racing, Vickie peered out around the corner again.

Mr. Lucre was bending over the fallen principal. "Stay calm," Vickie heard him say to himself. "Don't panic."

He straightened up. He cupped his hands to his mouth. *"Principal down!"* he shouted. *"Heeelp!"*

It was then that Vickie saw the skates and realized what she'd done. There they were, in plain view. Evidence.

She hadn't saved Maria after all.

"Principal?" muttered Maria.

Without giving herself time to think about what could

happen, Vickie pushed Maria back. "Stay right here!" she ordered. "Don't move!"

She ran back out into the hall and toward Mr. Lucre. Doors opened as she ran. Voices rose.

But she reached Mr. Lucre first. "Mr. Lucre! You called for help! What happened?" she asked.

The assistant principal pointed down at the inert body of Dr. Morthouse. Then he began to wring his hands.

"She's fallen," he moaned. "I can't get her up."

Teachers and students began to converge on them.

"You did right not to move her," said Vickie. "I'll go call for help." She stepped back. She bent down, keeping her eyes on Mr. Lucre.

He wasn't watching her. He was staring at the ceiling. He was staring at the floor.

"Mr. Lucre!" cried a teacher's voice, and Ms. Camp, an English teacher, came hurrying toward them.

But Ms. Camp wasn't watching Vickie either. Vickie bent lower, lower, never taking her gaze off the panicky assistant principal.

Her hands touched the skates.

With a jerk, like a body out of a coffin, Dr. Morthouse sat up. She swung around to face Vickie. Her eyes narrowed. Her mouth opened. Something silver, like a fang, flashed in her mouth.

"Drop those skates!" she snarled.

CHAPTER
4

Vickie dropped the skates.

She ran.

A wave of teachers and students streamed past her on either side. They surrounded Dr. Morthouse.

"Hey, Vickie!" she thought she heard Dr. Morthouse say.

But she didn't wait around to find out.

She made a wide, high-speed turn around the corner of the hall. "Sorry!" she burst out. "I'll get your skates back, Maria, I . . ."

Her voice trailed off. The only thing in the hall was Maria's backpack.

Maria was gone.

Maria stared at her face in the mirror. She reached up to touch her forehead. A faint lump had appeared under the skin. What had happened, exactly?

She couldn't remember. Was she having amnesia? It was something to do with skates.

She'd been skating in the hall.

She closed her eyes, opened them again, met her own eyes in the mirror. She groaned.

No. It wasn't possible. She couldn't have been skating in the halls.

She'd had a bad fall and her head hurt. That explained it. She was dizzy. She wasn't herself.

The door opened.

"Are you all right?" an anxious voice asked. "Do you need a doctor?"

As the students shuffled toward their homerooms, the intercom crackled to life. It gave an ear-shattering shriek, garbled several words, then settled down.

". . . five extra minutes to get to class this morning due to a slight disruption in the schedule. Teachers: Do not issue tardy passes. Thank you."

"Was that Dr. Morthouse?" asked Stacey. Park, who'd fallen into step beside her, snorted.

"Yeah, right," he said. "Like Dr. Morthouse would give us five extra minutes to get to class when she could hand out nine million extra tardy passes instead."

"You're right." Stacey picked up her pace. "It's probably her sick idea of an April Fools' joke. No way I'm taking five extra minutes to get *anywhere*."

* * *

"I don't need a doctor!"

Vickie held up her hands. "Okay, okay! You don't have to get so excited."

Poor Maria, thought Vickie. She was upset. And she had every reason to be. Vickie had left Maria's brand-new in-line skates in Dr. Morthouse's clutches.

No wonder Maria had run into the bathroom. Vickie had just found her hanging over the sink, her face pale, her eyes wide.

"But I have to say, you don't look so good, you know? Put some more water on your face." Vickie wrenched one of the sandpaper-quality paper towels from the dispenser, softened it slightly by soaking it under the faucet, then began rubbing Maria's face.

With something suspiciously like a snarl, Maria slapped the paper towel away. "Don't touch me!"

"Maria, I'm sorry! What can I say? I was trying to save you from Dr. Morthouse. I didn't mean to leave your skates."

"Dr. Morthouse," said Maria. She put one hand up and smoothed her bangs down over the lump on her forehead. Then she said, "What, exactly, happened? If you don't mind telling me?"

The sarcastic tone made Vickie wince. "You don't remember?"

"Would I have asked if I remembered?" Maria practically shouted. She spun around to face Vickie. Her eyes blazed. Her mouth opened in a spooky snarl.

In spite of herself, Vickie stepped back. She held up her hands. "Okay, okay. We, uh, you and I, went up to the second floor back of the school to try the hall out with our wheels."

"What!"

"You know, your blades, my skateboard."

"In the school?"

"Shhh. Keep your voice down! It was before school, see, so we knew we were pretty safe. Only on our last run, you high-sided the corner and kept going down the hall. By the time I got there, you'd crashed into Dr. Morthouse."

"Dr. Morthouse?"

Vickie winced. "What? Are you calling her or something? Stop shouting."

"I am not shouting."

"Well, you're talking pretty loud."

"Loudly."

"Huh?"

"The correct word is loudly."

"Wow," Vickie breathed. "You really did take a knock on the head, Maria."

"Maria Medina, sixth grade. Accomplices are Stacey Carter, Vickie Wheilson."

Considerably startled, Vickie said, "Maria, I didn't say you'd lost your mind. Stop that. You're giving me the creeps. You sound like one of those guys in charge of the prisons in the old movies."

Maria turned back to the mirror. She leaned forward until her nose was almost touching the glass.

The announcement giving the students five minutes' grace crackled over the loudspeaker.

Maria jerked away from the mirror and whipped around to face Vickie. She looked puzzled. Angry. Weird.

But Vickie had already turned to pick up Maria's pack and hand it to her.

"Cool," said Vickie. "This may be our lucky day after all. Maybe it won't be so hard to get your blades back."

Maria stood in the doorway of the classroom, frowning. From behind, Vickie gave her a little push, frowning herself. Maria had clearly been shaken by that fall. Maybe she should see a doctor. Or a nurse.

But the last school nurse had disappeared under mysterious circumstances, never to be seen again, long before Vickie's time.

Rumor had it that she'd taken a job at a very strange summer camp.

Vickie shook her head and said, "See you later, Maria."

Maria didn't answer. She stepped into the classroom and peered around. The students were rowdy. The homeroom teacher was reading, clearly uninterested in trying to call for order until the bell rang.

Stacey Carter, sitting near the back of the room as usual, waved her arm wildly. Then she pointed to the empty desk next to her.

Feeling relieved somehow, Maria walked forward and slid into the desk by Stacey.

"Five minutes and no tardy slips," Stacey crowed. "Can you believe it?

"Scarcely," said Maria.

"I mean, I thought it was Sick Morthouse's sick idea of an April Fools' joke, but it's for real. And didja hear what happened?"

"Sick Morthouse?"

"Dr. Doom, principal of Graveyard School, almost left the planet this morning." Stacey stopped. "Maria, are you all right?"

Maria looked around the room. What was wrong with this picture? What was wrong with her? Why did she feel so sick, as if her skin was too tight?

"I'm fine," she said aloud.

"Good. So I hear Dr. Doom got chopped this morning. Some kid ran into her and took her out. Isn't that excellent?"

"Was she hurt?" asked Maria.

"No. Our principal comes from the dark side, remember? She's indestructible."

The last bell rang before Maria could answer.

She felt a little better. At least the crash hadn't killed Dr. Morthouse.

The teacher walked over to close the door of the classroom—and froze.

A familiar figure shot past her and spun once around

the desk. The figure paused at the corner, and her gaze swept the room.

For one moment, Dr. Morthouse's steely gray eyes met Maria's dark brown ones. Then, suit and all, the principal pushed off and out of the room.

"Outta my way," she shouted at the teacher as she elbowed through the door. "I'm trying to think!"

Then she was gone in a whir of wheels down the hall.

The homeroom teacher staggered back and collapsed in her chair.

No one moved. No one spoke.

It was all too horrible to be true.

But it was true.

It was Dr. Morthouse. And she was wearing Maria's blades.

CHAPTER
5

Without realizing what she was doing, Maria stood up. Her eyes were wide with shock.

Her heart was pounding.

It was the most horrifying sight she had ever seen.

"No!" shouted Maria. *"Noooooo!"* She put her hand to her mouth and ran out of the room.

Dr. Morthouse skated on, up and down the halls. She clomped up the stairs and bladed, then slid down the banisters and bladed some more.

Her long legs gave her awesome speed. The wheels of the blades made her tower over everyone else.

She liked that. She also liked the way they shrank back as she went by. She liked the mouths dropping open, the whimpers of fear and shock.

Who cared if she was losing her mind? This was the way to go.

*   *   *

"Maria, you've got to come out of the bathroom sometime."

Maria didn't answer. She sat on the toilet lid, her knees drawn up. She was thinking.

Stacey hammered on the stall door. "I'm not coming in there after you! These floors are gross."

The end-of-the-period bell rang.

Stacey said, "I gotta go get my pack. You better be out of there when I get back."

Students came and went. Toilets flushed. Bits of conversation swirled around Maria.

"On blades! Can you believe it?"

"I heard she took them away from Maria!"

"Poor Maria . . ."

". . . April Fools'?"

"Are you kidding? Mad Dog Morthouse doesn't even like for us to get Christmas holidays. She'd cancel summer if she could."

Vicious laughter.

Maria frowned.

"Someone should tell her to put on guards, at least. She's gonna kill herself in the halls."

"Nah. No way. Dr. Doom isn't even human."

More laughter.

The warning bell rang. Dawdling till the last minute, the bathroom crowd gradually began to thin out.

Maria—or what *looked* like Maria—tilted her head back and took a deep breath. Her thoughts were clearing

31

now. She could have gotten up again, looked in the mirror to make sure.

But she didn't need to. Instead, she looked down at her hands, at the front of her rugby shirt, at her blue-jeaned legs and her sneakered feet.

How had it happened? What was she going to do? She had been Dr. Morthouse, the principal—but she was just a kid now. It felt terrible.

Stacey pounded on the stall door. "Maria, are you still in there?" she asked.

"No," said Maria's voice.

Vickie said, "Yes you are. Listen, I saw what happened. I'm sorry about your skates. But I don't think she knows they're yours. That's good."

Maria didn't answer.

"Vickie told me what happened, Maria," Stacey said. "Listen, I think it's awesome that you're the one who took Morthouse out. I mean, it's not like you hurt her. In fact, I think it's done her a lot of good, don't you?"

Vickie whispered, *"What?"*

"Shhh," whispered Stacey. Then she raised her voice again. "We'll get your blades back, I promise. But you'd better come out. Or you'll get a tardy pass and have to go to the principal's office."

"Yeah. And even if you did unchain her brain when you two wiped out, and even if she doesn't know what's going on, you don't want to have to go to Dr. Morthouse's *office,* do you?" Vickie could be very logical, very persuasive.

Vickie's face, upside down, appeared beneath the stall door.

Maria stared down at her.

"Hey! You're upside down!" said Vickie.

"Feeble, Vick," Stacey said.

But Maria smiled.

Vickie's face disappeared abruptly.

Silence. Then, slowly, Maria lowered one foot off the toilet, and then the other. She stood up.

"I . . ." Her voice sounded funny. Gravelly. But emotional. Not a pretty combination. She cleared her throat. "I guess you're right," she said.

She pushed open the door.

There they stood. Her good friend Vickie. Her best friend, Stacey. Nice kids.

Nice kids. What was she thinking?

"You don't look so good," said Stacey. "Maybe you should go to the office."

"No!" yelped Maria.

"I mean, and call your mother or father. Go home."

Maria shook her head. Then she said, "We'll be late to class. We'd better go." She got between them. Safety in numbers.

Vickie went into math class.

Stacey went into science class.

Maria stopped. She pictured the class schedule.

"Ah," she said aloud. She went a little farther down the hall to language arts. Inside, with her back safely against the wall, she'd try to think. Try to figure out what had happened to her.

And what she was going to do about it.

Dr. Morthouse—or what looked like Dr. Morthouse—swung into the office and snatched the microphone from Mr. Kinderbane, the office manager. "Hello!" she shouted into the intercom. "Extra dessert for everyone at lunch today."

She tossed the microphone back at the startled office manager and skated into her office. She fell into her chair and swung her blade-clad feet up onto the desk.

This was living. Why hadn't she ever done this before? So what if people were looking at her strangely? So what if she was having a little memory problem? She'd had a bad fall. Hadn't Mr. Lucre said so? Hit her head. Happened all the time.

It was cool. She could handle it.

She frowned as a smell wafted through the door. She punched a button on the phone. "Excuse me, Mr. Kinderbane?"

"Yes, Dr. Morthouse?"

"What is that disgusting smell?"

"Smell . . . oh. Lunch," said Mr. Kinderbane.

Dr. Morthouse hung up the phone. Lunch? That was lunch?

No way was she going to eat something that smelled like that. She picked up the phone again, buzzed Mr. Kinderbane.

3 4

"Get me the phone number for Pizza Park," she ordered. She paused, then added, "And have all the teachers in the school meet me in the large conference room at twelve-thirty sharp today."

"Double dessert!" crowed Jaws Bennett. He forked a wad of chocolate pudding cake into his mouth with a bite of chicken noodle surprise and chewed with gusto.

"Jaws, tell me," asked Stacey in a conversational tone. "Have you ever *really* eaten roadkill?"

"Arrmmm," said Jaws, his mouth full.

"He hasn't," translated Park. "But he would."

"I almost believe it's true," said Stacey, as Jaws continued to devour the school lunch with double dessert.

She poked her fork into the gelatinous mass of noodles and chicken. She'd had worse lunches. Much worse.

Maria, Stacey noticed, was eating with almost as much gusto as Jaws.

"Feeling better?" Stacey asked.

"Delicious," said Maria.

"Huh?"

"Nutritious, wholesome, and economical," continued Maria.

"Maria!"

"I guess I still have a little bit of a headache," said Maria.

"I guess," said Stacey. "This lunch is gross. Just like all the others.

"IagreewiMaria," Jaws mumbled.

They ignored him.

Maria put down her fork. She was going to have to be careful. Watch her back. Watch her mouth.

At that moment the loudspeaker crackled to life.

"But Dr. Morthouse!" they heard Mr. Lucre wail.

Then Dr. Morthouse's voice sang out, "Attention, attention. All teachers who have not reported to the large conference room, do so at once. Now!"

The few remaining teachers in the lunchroom exchanged startled glances.

"Now!" cried Dr. Morthouse in a strangely gleeful voice.

Slowly, reluctantly, the handful of teachers began to walk toward the door. With each step they took, the noise level in the lunchroom seemed to rise.

Bent said, "All the teachers. Cool. We are about to have some fun."

Skate muttered, "Trouble."

The doors of the lunchroom closed.

A geyser of food flew toward the ceiling. Across the room, Skip Wolfson jumped up on the chair, cupped his hands around his mouth, and began to howl.

Algie began to gather the dried-up oranges that had been served with their lunches and juggle them.

Someone shrieked. A chair fell over. Then another.

Then a table went.

Behind the serving counter, the lunchroom staff exchanged worried glances.

A food fight broke out between former class president Jason Dunnbar and former skateboarder Eddie Hoover. Eddie seized one of the second-graders to use as a shield.

The second-grader's fourth-grade sister mashed her chocolate pudding cake into Eddie's hair.

Civilization broke down in three minutes flat.

The lunchroom staff fled.

Then Maria rose to her feet. "What's that?" she choked out.

No one heard her. The noise was too loud, the insane energy too overwhelming.

Disbelievingly, Maria walked over to the windows on one side of the lunchroom—not the ones that looked up the hill to the old graveyard, but the ones that looked out over the side parking lot.

She hadn't believed her eyes. But it was true. A pizza delivery truck was parked at the side door of the school near the large conference room. And two guys in silly hats and shirts with pizza stains on them were unloading boxes and boxes of pizza and soda.

That's where all the teachers are, thought Maria. *Eating pizza while Grove Hill School burns.*

She turned. Kids were sliding up and down the lunchroom in the slick of noodles made by upended trays and tables.

"We gotta get out of here!" she heard Stacey shout.

Maria charged forward. She pushed several much larger kids aside. She snarled so ferociously at Jason that he fell back in confusion.

An orange sailed by her ear. But it was as if she were surrounded by an invisible shield. Nothing touched her. She reached the door of the lunchroom unscathed, only to realize that someone was tugging on her arm.

Turning, she saw Stacey and Vickie standing behind her. They hadn't been so lucky. As they stood there, another figure reeled up. Stacey and Vickie were tattooed with noodles, speckled with chocolate, dotted with crumbs. But the person who reeled up to them was clothed in food.

"Kill them!" Polly Hannah shrieked, flinging noodles far and wide as she waved her arms and pointed. "Kill them!"

"Maria, where are you going?" asked Stacey.

"This has gone far enough," Maria answered. "This is a job for Dr. Morthouse!"

CHAPTER

6

Stacey, Vickie, and Polly fell back in shock.

"Dr . . . Dr. Morthouse?" Vickie managed to say at last. "You're going to go *get* Dr. Morthouse? Like, voluntarily?"

"Yes."

"Don't!" pleaded Stacey. "Don't do it. You don't know what could happen! Sure she's been nice today, but she's . . . she's not herself. She could turn on you!"

"Like a rabid dog," said Vickie. "Tear you limb from limb. Bury you in the basement. Suspend you for life." Vickie took a deep breath. "Wipe you out forever. End your miserable existence. Turn you into hallkill in the schoolhouse of life."

"I get your point. I don't believe Dr. Morthouse would resort to such drastic extremes." Maria smiled, and Stacey and Vickie both frowned. An involuntary shudder ran through Vickie. Where had she seen that smile before?

Maria added, "Unless, of course, she had good cause."

Still frowning, Stacey said, "Dr. Morthouse doesn't need good cause, Maria! You know that. She's wacked to the max. Twisted to the treetops. The ghoul who rules, y'know."

"What has she ever done to you?" asked Maria.

"Ha, ha, April Fools'," said Stacey impatiently. "*Not* funny."

"That's what this is!" exclaimed Vickie in relief. "Wow, you really had me going. I thought you were going to go get Mad Dog Morthouse."

This time Maria didn't smile. She just said, "Pretend it's the second day of April. Because I'm not fooling. I'm going to get the person in charge and straighten this mess out."

She turned and pushed her way out of the lunchroom.

The halls were empty. Behind her, the lunchroom sounded as if the windows were about to explode outward from the noise. Was this how Graveyard, no, Grove Hill School was going to end? In a food fight, while the teachers partied on pizza?

Maria's face was grim as she stormed down the halls. Anyone passing her would have been startled at how ferociously her black brows were drawn together, at how sharp her teeth seemed beneath her drawn-back lips. They might also have noticed that not only were Maria's bangs standing up, but the hair all over her head was on end, like a wild animal's.

But no one saw her, although behind some of the classroom doors, where the kids who hadn't gone to lunch had been left when their teachers had been commandeered by the principal, the noise level almost equaled that of the lunchroom.

Maria winced at the sounds of desks toppling, erasers flying, and worst of all, chalk squeaking on blackboards.

"Animals," she muttered. "Animals."

As she approached the large conference room, the noise grew louder. And louder. It drowned out all the other noise in the hall. It was even more explosive than the sounds rocking the lunchroom.

"So then I said to the little twerp, 'Shut up or I'll glue your other hand to the blackboard,' " a teacher's voice said, followed by uproarious laughter and raucous cheers.

". . . give me an *i!*"

"IIIII!"

"Give me an *o!*"

"OOOO!"

"Give me an *n!*"

"NNNN!"

"What's it spell?"

"Detention!"

"Louder!"

"Detention!"

"I can't hear you . . ."

"DETENTION!"

Maria burst through the door of the large conference room, swinging it open with a bang.

No one even noticed. Teachers were dancing on the tables. Teachers were bouncing on the chairs. Teachers were hurling pizza across the room and playing Catch the Pepperoni with their mouths. They were laughing and screaming and partying on.

It was a horrible, horrible sight.

"Stop it! Stop it at once!" shouted Maria.

"Hey, look!" a teacher shouted. "It's a student!"

Half a dozen teachers turned to look. Then one of them screamed, "April Fools'!" and they all rocked with laughter.

Scanning the room desperately, Maria at last spotted Dr. Morthouse's figure. She had lined up a row of chairs and pizza boxes and was skating in and out among the chairs and leaping over the pizza boxes. Mr. Lucre, his hair completely awry so that his bald spot shined brightly, was applauding each maneuver.

"Brilliant! Excellent work, Morty."

Morty? *Morty?*

"Three cheers for Morty!" someone else cried.

Cheers broke out around the room. Dr. Morthouse swooped around the last chair and spun gracefully to bow to the room at large.

"Pizza on, dudes!" she screamed, and everyone applauded.

Dodging a rain of pepperoni and a shower of soda from a soda fight, Maria reached Dr. Morthouse at last.

She clamped her hand on the principal's arm.

The principal jumped and almost lost her balance. Maria jerked her upright.

"Look at me," she snarled.

Dr. Morthouse looked down at Maria. Maria surveyed the principal.

She was not the woman she had been that morning. Her pearls were slung backward around her neck. Tufts of hair sprang out from her bun, which looked as if it had fallen and would never get up. Her trim gray pantsuit had been rolled up at the knees, and she had taken off her silk scarf and tied it around her waist. Worst of all, she'd unbuttoned the ruffled high-necked blouse one whole button.

Maria blanched. "Get a grip," she ordered.

Dr. Morthouse gave Maria a wild-eyed look. "W-Who are you?"

"You don't know? You don't know who I am? Take a good look!" Maria grasped a fistful of the lapel of the gray jacket and dragged Dr. Morthouse down, down, down, until her eyes were level with Maria's.

"Well!" said Maria. "Well?"

"Morty! Need some help here?" asked a nervously jovial voice.

"Say no," ordered Maria.

Staring deep into Maria's eyes, Dr. Morthouse said, "N-No. Thank you."

"You're sure?"

"Uh, just go have a good time, Hannibal. I'll be right there. Just a, uh, little student conference."

"Good," said Maria.

Dr. Morthouse swallowed hard. Then suddenly she tried to straighten up. "What do you think you're doing, little girl?'' she said. ''I'm the principal. I could have you expelled for this.''

''Could you?'' asked Maria coolly.

Dr. Morthouse giggled.

A shudder ran through Maria. She did what she always did in times of stress.

She smiled.

Dr. Morthouse's eyes widened. They rolled wildly in her head. She skated backward so suddenly that Maria almost fell.

''*No!*'' screamed Dr. Morthouse. ''Get away from me! Get away!''

CHAPTER
7

"What are you doing to Dr. Morthouse?'' shouted a voice.

Maria said, "You know who I am, don't you, *Dr. Morthouse*?''

The tall figure in the gray pantsuit turned and roller-sprinted from the conference room.

She left the door open.

A wave of noise poured in from the halls. The food fight had escaped from the lunchroom. So had the students. Attracted by the commotion, other students were streaming from the classrooms to join in the chaos.

Heads will roll for this, thought Maria grimly. But not without pleasure in the thought.

The noise of hundreds of out-of-their-tiny-minds kids gradually overwhelmed the noise of a much smaller number of rowdy teachers. The pizza party ground to a halt. Heads turned toward the open door.

One teacher muttered, "Oh no!"

"Oh dear, oh dear," said Mr. Lucre.

Maria couldn't stand it any longer. "Do something!" she shouted.

Every eye in the room turned toward her. Then Maria's homeroom teacher said sternly, "Maria! What are you doing in the teachers' conference room?"

Someone said under his breath, "Detention."

Maria looked at the pizza-smeared room. She looked out at the student-infested halls.

She took a deep breath and did something she hadn't done in years and years.

She ran.

Dr. Morthouse's tall form went through the students like a hot knife through butter. From first-graders to sixth-graders, they melted away, slid out of sight, sought the safety of their classrooms as the principal rolled past them. The brigade of teachers pouring out of the large conference room, firing words like *detention, suspension, homework*, and *parent-teacher conference*, did the rest.

Order began to return to Graveyard School.

Dr. Morthouse skated on, shoving the unfortunate few who didn't get out of the way fast enough back against the lockers. She took terrible risks, banking corners on one foot, leaping scattered books at a single bound.

She managed to stay well ahead of Maria.

But she wasn't able to lose her.

Maria seemed to know by heart every turn, every dodge, every hidden staircase. She ran, but unlike Dr. Morthouse's, her pace had no urgency. She was hunting something she clearly believed she was sure to catch.

And when Dr. Morthouse ducked down a flight of stairs near the back of the school, Maria slowed her steps to a jog. A nasty glow lit up her eyes.

No need to hurry now. "I know something you don't know," she singsonged like a first-grader.

The skates clattered down the stairs. Stopped. Something thumped hard against something even harder.

"Oww," muttered a voice.

Maria reached the top of the stairs. She looked down at the figure that was pulling urgently at the broken emergency exit, scheduled to be fixed but not until later that afternoon.

"Having a problem?" she asked. She smiled.

And Dr. Morthouse began to scream.

Feeling the teacher's gimlet eye on her, Vickie shifted her attention away from Maria's empty desk. She stared down at her open book. But she wasn't thinking about her schoolwork. She was wondering where Maria had disappeared to.

She sighed. At least Maria wasn't sitting in class, wishing she was out laying wicked wheels along some smooth surface.

Remembering their conversation the day before up on Graveyard Hill, Vickie wondered what it would be like to switch bodies with Dr. Morthouse.

Ugh.

Or Polly Hannah.

Double ugh.

What was it like to be like Polly Hannah?

Thinking of the way Polly sat in class, Vickie put her feet together and folded her hands on her desk. She straightened her spine. As an afterthought, she smoothed, as best she could, her spiky red hair.

For a whole minute she sat like that. She tried to pretend she really was Polly Hannah. Tried to imagine that her body was wrapped in a flowered dress, stockings, and flat shoes with bows on the toes. It made her itch just to think about it.

"Stop that," ordered the principal.

Maria choked off the sound in midscream.

The principal folded her arms and looked down the stairs at the figure backed into the corner below. "Well, well, well," she said. "What have you got to say for yourself, young lady?"

Why had she ever thought it would be interesting to be Dr. Morthouse? What had she done to deserve this? How had it happened?

How had she, Maria Medina, ordinary sixth-grader, switched bodies with Dr. Morthouse, the principal from the dark side?

"Well?" said the voice above her. "I'm waiting."

At first Maria hadn't been sure what had happened. She'd been groggy. Hadn't been able to breathe. Then Mr. Lucre's face had loomed up in front of her.

My helmet came off, she'd thought groggily. *I hit my head and it knocked me out. Did something to my hearing, too.*

But it wasn't her hearing that had been affected.

It was her whole body, as she'd discovered when Mr. Lucre began helping her to her feet. She stood up, up, up. Suddenly she was towering over the assistant principal. Towering over the other teachers.

Dwarfing the students.

The cowering students.

And why was Vickie acting so strangely, sneaking up like that to try to grab her skates?

Then she'd looked down and seen her legs. Her long, gray-pantsuit-wrapped legs. Had heard Mr. Lucre say urgently, in her ear, "Dr. Morthouse? Are you all right?"

She'd turned to stare at Mr. Lucre. Yes. He was talking to her. To Maria.

Only I don't look like Maria anymore, she'd realized.

I look like Dr. Morthouse.

Vickie had picked up the skates. Desperate, Maria

had lunged for the only thing left she was sure of in an insane world.

"Drop those skates," she had snarled.

A shadow had fallen across her, and she'd looked up.

She'd shrunk back, wishing she could force herself into the wall.

"I can't heeeearr youuuuu," the principal had said.

They'd led her away, dazed and confused. Helped her into the principal's chair in the principal's office. Mr. Kinderbane had brought her coffee.

Yuck.

When he'd asked her if something was wrong with the coffee and she'd said, without thinking, "I want a Coke," he'd shot away and had returned moments later with a soda.

"Just rest," he'd said. "I'll see that you're not disturbed."

But, staring at the Coke that the office manager had placed almost reverently in her hand, Maria had realized that being turned into Dr. Morthouse might not be quite as horrible as she'd thought.

That was when she'd thought of the pizza.

Remembering the pizza, she smiled.

"What's so funny?" a voice snarled from inches away, jerking her back to the terrifying present.

Her own face appeared in front of her.

Maria shrieked. It was worse than horrible.

It was the mirror image from a nightmare. She

stared into her own eyes. She watched her lips part in a terrifying smile.

It was all too sickeningly true. She and Dr. Morthouse had switched bodies. She, Maria, was trapped in Dr. Morthouse's body.

And Dr. Morthouse was trapped in hers.

Dr. Morthouse, the real Dr. Morthouse inside Maria's body, leaned closer. "Give me back my body," she whispered. "Give it back to me, or I'll—"

"Dr. Morthouse? Dr. Morthouse? Is everything in order?"

Dr. Morthouse looked over her shoulder. Maria looked up. But it was to Maria that Mr. Lucre was talking as he clomped down the stairs. "Not having a problem with this student, are you?" he continued, grabbing Dr. Morthouse by the shoulder in a grip that made her bare her teeth in a silent snarl.

Mr. Lucre looked at Maria. Maria straightened up slowly. For once, Mr. Lucre had saved a student's life. She wondered how he'd feel about making such a big mistake.

Dr. Morthouse squirmed in Mr. Lucre's grasp. "Let go of me," she ordered.

"Calm down, young lady," said Mr. Lucre with false heartiness.

Maria straightened up. She put her hand up and pushed the hair that had fallen down on her forehead straight back. She smoothed the lapels of the gray jacket.

The image of Mr. Kinderbane rushing out to get the

Coke flashed before her eyes. Not only had Mr. Lucre saved her life, but he'd made her realize something important.

Something very, very important.

No one knew she wasn't Dr. Morthouse. She, Maria Medina, could do whatever she wanted.

And there was no way Dr. Morthouse, trapped in a sixth-grader's body, could stop her.

Maria smiled sweetly. "As a matter of fact, Mr. Lucre, you could take this student back to class. I caught her trying to sneak out the emergency exit."

"Oh dear. How dreadful! Shall I write up a detention?"

"I'll take the matter under consideration," promised Maria, giving Dr. Morthouse a triumphant look.

Dr. Morthouse snarled. Seeing her own face look so awful, Maria felt slightly sick. But what could she do?

She might as well make the best of a bad situation.

"I'll be in my office," said Maria.

"I'll be *back,*" promised Dr. Morthouse as Mr. Lucre marched her away.

Vickie looked up as Mr. Lucre marched Maria into class, one hand clamped tightly on her shoulder. Everyone else looked up, too.

"We've been a naughty girl, trying to skip our classes. I guess all the excitement today has gone to our head," said Mr. Lucre.

Maria stalked to the nearest desk and sat down.

"Maria, go to your own desk," said the teacher, frowning. "Thank you, Mr. Lucre."

Vickie motioned to Maria as she stood up and looked around in an almost puzzled way.

Slowly, almost tentatively, Maria walked down the aisle and slid into the seat next to Vickie.

"Where're your books?" asked Vickie. "Didn't you go to your locker?"

"No."

Sliding her own book to the side of the desk near Maria, Vickie said, "Here. You can use mine. If you can stay awake. Boring."

"Really." Maria flashed Vickie a look that made her wince.

Geez, Vickie thought, *Maria is still angry about losing her skates.*

Of course, who could blame her, after what had happened?

"Hey. Pssst. Maria."

Maria gave Vickie another one of those unnerving looks. For a second she didn't seem like Maria at all. Something about Maria reminded Vickie of . . . of . . .

But Vickie couldn't quite figure out who Maria looked like.

"Maria, listen, I'll get your skates back. Tonight. Even if I have to go to Dr. Morthouse's to do it."

That got Maria's attention. She whipped around so fast she was almost a blur, like a striking snake. Involuntarily Vickie jerked back.

53

"To Dr. Morthouse's? But you don't know where I—er, Dr. Morthouse lives."

"No problem," said Vickie with a nonchalance she didn't feel. "Easy. We just follow her home. I call my house and say I'm having dinner at your house, you call my house and say you're having dinner at mine. Then we go on a search-and-recover mission."

"Follow me—Morthouse home?" Maria asked tentatively. It scared her more than she liked to admit.

CHAPTER
8

Maria kept thinking her body was going to change back. She sat in Dr. Morthouse's office, frozen in the big chair behind the desk, waiting. But nothing happened.

And no way could she figure out what *had* happened. What had gone so terribly, terribly wrong.

One minute she'd been happily skating down the hall. The next minute, *bam*. She'd been lying on the floor in a Dr. Morthouse suit.

It could be worse, thought Maria. *I could be trapped in here with Dr. Morthouse. Yecch. Detention to the max.*

Of course, having Dr. Morthouse on the loose in her— Maria's—body wasn't much better.

The door of the office opened. Maria jumped a mile, then tried to pretend she was just standing up.

"Day's end," said Mr. Kinderbane. He looked down at the skates Maria was still wearing, but didn't comment.

Instead he said, "Are you staying late? Do you want me to stay too?"

Maria looked around. Stay? In Dr. Morthouse's office after the school was closed? Wait for the real Dr. Morthouse to come sneaking up on her?

No way.

She was trying to think fast when her eyes lit on the big, black briefcase on top of one of the file cabinets. She reached up and grabbed it.

Mr. Kinderbane nodded. "See you tomorrow," he said.

"Uh, okay," said Maria.

The office manager frowned and left.

It wasn't a real briefcase, Maria saw. Just a briefcase-shaped purse. Did she dare?

Heart pounding, she slid back the latch and slowly opened the principal's handbag.

She peered down inside.

"Bor-ing," she said.

The bag contained a wallet, a checkbook, a datebook, two pens, one pencil, a strange book of foreign stamps with ghoulish figures on them, an electric bill addressed to Dr. Morthouse, and a collection of loose change at the bottom along with three sets of keys. One was a set of car keys. One was clearly labeled OFFICE. The other didn't look like an ordinary set of keys at all. It was two big iron keys, each ornately decorated on one end, heavy and almost the size of her hand, caught together on a plain key ring.

Not knowing what else to do, Maria took the office keys out and locked the office door behind her as she left. The halls of the school were deserted. She'd been in the school before when the halls were deserted. Then it had been sort of interesting.

Now it made her nervous. She skated along, keeping a sharp eye out for a certain figure that might be lurking beside a water fountain or around a door, ready to spring out and get her.

Her own.

Maria had bested Dr. Morthouse once, but even though she was now twice as big as the principal—*was*, outwardly, the principal—she didn't trust Dr. Morthouse.

Dr. Morthouse would get her body back.

Or die trying.

I'm too young to die, thought Maria confusedly.

She reached the front door and locked it behind her. At the top of the huge flight of stairs leading up to the school, she looked carefully around.

The coast was clear.

But what was she going to do now?

She had Dr. Morthouse's car keys. Driving the principal's car might be fun.

It was a very tempting thought. But Maria put it out of her mind at last. The day had been weird enough without taking any more chances. Besides, she still had her blades. They would take her anywhere.

She walked carefully down the steps and stopped

5 7

again. She had her blades and they would take her anywhere, but where did she want to go?

She couldn't go home. It was too early for dinner. Somehow she didn't think she'd be welcome at the park or up on Skateboard Hill. And she didn't feel like going to the mall to shop, much as Dr. Morthouse, in Maria's opinion, needed a complete fashion makeover.

Or at least a couple of rugby shirts and a pair of jeans. Maria sighed.

Then she remembered Dr. Morthouse's purse. She opened it again. She took out the wallet. She opened it.

The wallet was empty except for a sheaf of bills in the back. No credit cards. No driver's license. No video card. Nothing.

Weird.

Maria flipped open the checkbook. Dr. Morthouse's name was stamped across the top: DR. MORTHOUSE.

That was it. No first name. No address.

Weirder.

Then she remembered the envelope. The utility bill had a zero reading and a notice suggesting that the power company come to check Dr. Morthouse's meter to see if it was functioning properly. But Maria wasn't interested in that. What she was interested in was the address on the front.

Dr. Morthouse's address. 13 MISSING LANE, it read.

There. Now she knew where to go.

Home. Dr. Morthouse's home. Where else could she go?

She closed the purse and, clutching the envelope, skated slowly away from the school.

Vickie crawled out from under the shrubbery at the side of the road that ran past the school. She dropped her board on the ground.

"Wait for me," panted Dr.-Morthouse-in-Maria's-body.

"Oh. Right." Vickie picked up her board again. She'd forgotten that Maria didn't have wheels—thanks to her. "C'mon. Dr. Morthouse is getting away."

Vickie broke into a trot. A moment later Maria fell in beside her.

"She's still wearing your blades, Maria. Can you believe it?"

"That's not all of mine she's wearing," Vickie thought she heard Maria mutter.

"Huh?" Vickie said.

"Nothing."

"I thought she'd never leave the school. And what's with that envelope she's holding? Think she's going to mail a letter?"

"I think Dr. Morthouse very stupidly left a utility bill with her address on it in her purse," Maria panted beside Vickie.

"Yeah. Hmm. Whoa!" Vickie grabbed Maria and jerked her behind a hedge. "Look at that! She's talking to the letter carrier. Showing him the letter . . ."

"Smarter than I thought," Vickie heard Maria mutter.

The letter carrier scratched his head. Then he pulled a book out of his shoulder bag and flipped it open. The two of them bent over it. At last the letter carrier pointed vaguely.

Vickie heard Maria make a weird snarling sound.

They watched as the principal's tall figure took off once more, this time in the direction the letter carrier had pointed in.

Vickie and Maria—that is, Dr. Morthouse—took off, too.

They went up hills and down hills, into neighborhoods and out again. They skirted a skeazy strip mall.

"I don't like this, Maria," Vickie said. "Do you think she knows she's being followed? Do you think that's why she's going all over the place like this?"

"No."

"It's almost like she's lost."

"Yes."

Twice more they watched the principal ask directions. Then she wandered off again, with the two students in close pursuit.

Maria skated on. And on. And on. How come nobody knew where Dr. Morthouse lived? How come nobody had ever heard of Missing Lane?

She was tired. And hungry. And thirsty.

She slowed down, thinking of the money in Dr. Morthouse's wallet. Maybe she could borrow just a little and go over to that Chinese restaurant next to the flower shop and—

She almost skated into him as he emerged from the flower shop. He leaped back with an agitated cry. Then he gasped, "Dr. Morthouse!" Before Maria could stop him, he leaned forward and gave her a quick peck on the cheek.

It was Maria's turn to leap back with a gasp.

"But dear," said the man, "skates?"

Maria looked down. She looked up. This was a friend of Dr. Morthouse's? He appeared almost normal, tall and distinguished in a blue suit and dark tie, wings of silver hair on either side of his face.

"Uh, I took them away from a, uh, student."

"A principal of hidden talents." He laughed.

Maria thrust the envelope at him. "This address?" she said. "Do you . . . ?"

Before she could finish, the man said, "Tired of skating and want a ride home? Certainly, certainly. I'm finished here. Just a friendly business call." He put his hand under Maria's elbow and guided her across the parking lot.

He had a huge car. An enormous car. Maria got in and sank into the cushioned front seat gratefully.

Then she looked over her shoulder and realized that she was not alone.

A huge coffin was in the back of the car.

The car was a hearse.

CHAPTER
9

"This is unbelievable!" cried Dr. Morthouse-Maria, springing up from behind the pickup truck where she and Vickie had been hiding.

"Totally!" agreed Vickie. "I mean, she's getting into a hearse!"

The door of the hearse flew open. One bladed foot emerged. Then it disappeared back inside. The door slammed and the hearse began to pull away.

Vickie grabbed Maria, who seemed frozen to the spot in shock, and took off after it.

They wound slowly through several neighborhoods, each with houses bigger and older and set farther back from the street. The streets themselves grew darker under the ponderous branches of massive, twisted trees. Vickie soon had no idea where she was.

Then the car turned up a particularly dark and deserted-looking street. If there were houses, they weren't visible behind the overgrown hedges and thickly planted trees and shrubs.

"Good grief," panted Vickie. "This is like some weird horror movie setting."

"What are you talking about?"

"Well, Maria, it's not normal—Shhh!"

They stopped, hiding themselves easily behind the massive trunk of an old oak.

The street was a dead end. The hearse pulled to a stop in front of a pair of massive iron gates entwined with ivy.

"Here we are," said the funeral director. "Home sweet home. Thirteen Missing Lane."

Maria, who'd been sitting rigidly on the front seat the whole time, trying not to think of the coffin just over her left shoulder, managed to say, "Thanks."

"See you this weekend," said the director. Maria pushed the door open and slid out.

"See you this weekend," he said again.

"Uh, right," said Maria.

She watched until the hearse was out of sight. Until she was alone on the dark, dark street.

Then she turned to face her new home.

"I don't believe this!"

They watchéd as the principal fumbled with her keys, then pushed the big gate open with a screech of hinges.

The noise seemed to startle Dr. Morthouse, thought Vickie as she watched the principal jump, then peer nervously around.

It made Vickie jump, too. Beside her, she heard Maria mutter, "Get *over* it."

The principal slipped through the narrow opening of the gate and let it clang shut.

"That won't lock it," said Maria.

"I hope not," said Vickie. "I'd hate to have to try to climb over those walls. They're covered with thorns."

"Climbing roses," said Maria. "A very rare variety called Vampire's Blood."

"Ha, ha. I wouldn't be surprised if it was true," said Vickie.

When the principal had disappeared up the drive, the two of them crept forward. Vickie put her hand gingerly on the massive gate.

Just as Maria had predicted, the gate hadn't locked. Vickie pushed it open. The driveway ahead was smooth, made of pale red rocks, immaculately kept. It was lined with dark evergreens trimmed into fantastic shapes. In the gathering darkness the evergreens made twisted shadows on the gravel.

Vickie swallowed hard. She looked over her shoulder and said to the person she thought was Maria in what she hoped was a calm voice, "We're in."

Despite the ivy-covered gates and rose-veined walls that surrounded the house, Maria was surprised to see that what was inside the gate was neat and orderly. Over-whelming. Bizarre. But not neglected.

She gave a sigh of relief. For some reason, she'd expected Dr. Morthouse to live in a haunted house.

Of course, thought Maria as she walked down the flag-stone path lined with spikes of red grass, *any house Dr. Morthouse lived in would be haunted. By her.*

The front door was dark and massive. One of the other keys fit it perfectly, and it slid open with a screech that was an echo of the front gate's.

Maria stepped inside. She was standing in a dark hall-way. She reached out and groped for a light switch. But when she found it and flicked it, nothing happened.

She frowned.

Something slithered away at the far end of the dark tunnel that was the hall.

"H-Hello? Is anybody home?"

Maria had made jokes about Dr. Morthouse's secret life. But she'd never really thought about how the principal lived.

What if she had a husband? Kids? A big, vicious dog?

"Hello," she called again. "It's me. M-Morthouse. Dr. Morthouse . . . I'm home." She tried to make herself sound cheerful in a Morthouse kind of way.

No one answered. Nothing else slithered.

The house was as silent and dark as a tomb. The only light came from the narrow windows on either side of the door, pale rectangles of ghostly light from the fading af-ternoon.

Don't be ridiculous, Maria told herself. *Dr. Morthouse doesn't have a family.*

She went forward cautiously, squinting into the gloom. Ahead, a table suddenly loomed. Maria saw that on it, sticking up like spectral fingers, stood candles stuck in candlesticks. They were in different stages of melt. Running her fingers over the table, Maria found a book of matches, struck one, and lit the tallest candle.

The gloom turned into light and shadow. Maria raised the candlestick and began to explore her new home.

"Wow, good work, Maria," Vickie said. "How did you figure out there would be a spare key hidden under that cow's skull?"

"Puh-lease," rasped Dr. Morthouse. "Don't ask." She'd never liked kids. Being one wasn't improving her attitude.

Through the glass panels that flanked the front door, they'd watched the candlelight move down the hall and into a room. Now Dr. Morthouse inserted the key and opened the door.

She held it open slightly and motioned for Vickie to squeeze through.

"Cut me some room here, wouldja?" complained Vickie.

"Leave the skateboard," ordered Dr. Morthouse. "If I open the door any wider it's going to creak and give us away."

"How did you—"

"Go!" Dr. Morthouse pushed Vickie through the door. That was the problem with students these days. They had no respect for facts. They were nosy and asked questions and they *actually expected answers*.

Who did they think they were, anyway?

With a grunt Dr. Morthouse squeezed in after Vickie. She slipped past her and led the way to the candle-studded table and lit a candle.

"I wonder if she didn't pay her electric bill," said Vickie.

"No."

"Or if she just prefers the dark."

"Maybe." The candle was lit. Shielding it, Dr. Morthouse glided forward, trying to think of some way to shake Vickie off. She couldn't confront that dratted Maria Medina with Vickie hovering around her. The fewer people who knew about the situation, the better.

She paused. "Here." She handed Vickie the candle and pointed up the stairs.

"Hey, no way I'm letting us get separated! That's what they do in horror movies. Then the monster picks the people off one at a time."

"You're calling Dr. Morthouse a monster?" In spite of herself, Dr. Morthouse couldn't help the pleased smile that crossed her lips. Fortunately Vickie didn't notice. She was looking around nervously.

"Yes. No. Maybe. I don't know."

"Go upstairs and hide in her bedroom. When she takes her skates off, you can rush out and get them."

"I don't even know which bedroom is hers."

"The second one on the left at the top of the stairs," said Dr. Morthouse in an impatient whisper. "Now, go."

She gave Vickie a push.

"What about you? You'll be alone. *In the dark.*"

"I'll light another candle. If she takes the skates off down here, I'll grab them and then come get you."

She grabbed Vickie's arm and practically threw her toward the staircase.

"I don't like it."

"Just do it!"

The steel thread in Maria's voice was oddly familiar to Vickie. She found herself unable to resist it. Only later did she realize that the voice didn't sound like Maria's voice.

And only much, much later did she realize why.

She stumbled up the stairs. The thick carpeting absorbed the sound of her footsteps. The shadows seemed to swallow all the light.

When she got to the top she looked down. "How did you know which bedroom . . . ," she began in a loud whisper.

She stopped. The hall below was in complete darkness. Maria was nowhere to be seen.

CHAPTER
10

A dining room filled with dark polished wood furniture and tall, uncomfortable-looking chairs. A kitchen that looked like something from a magazine, all shiny-new and unused. Every window in the house, except for the two that flanked the front door, was heavily curtained or shuttered.

Something rustled in the air above her. Maria raised her candle and peered upward. But she could see nothing in the shadows that hung like storm clouds under the high ceilings.

None of the lights worked. Her skates rolled across polished wood, moved with a muffled thump across thick carpets.

A living room, full of more gloomy, uncomfortable-looking furniture. A study full of heavy books and a squat, malevolent-looking desk.

Weird, but not too bad, Maria decided. With real light, it would probably look ordinary.

She turned.

She flinched.

Had something slipped sideways into the gloom behind her?

Raising the candle again, she said, "H-Hello? Is anybody there?"

Once again, no one volunteered any information.

Quickly, as quickly as she could without causing the candle to blow out, Maria turned and hurried back out into the hall. The light passed over a telephone.

She suddenly remembered that she hadn't called home to say she would be late.

But what if Maria—Dr. Morthouse, that is—had gone home in her place? Maria frowned at the thought of the principal unleashed on her unsuspecting family.

I hope our cat rips her legs off, she thought spitefully.

Then she remembered that those legs were her legs, and took the wish back.

Her hand hovered uncertainly above the phone. At last she picked it up. To her surprise, it was working. She dialed. Her mother answered.

Her mother's hello didn't sound upset or worried. Trying to disguise her voice, Maria asked to speak to—Maria.

"Maria, stop that. You and Vickie are supposed to be doing homework, not playing childish games on the phone."

"Oh," said Maria.

Her mother laughed. "You didn't think I'd know my own daughter?"

"N-No," said Maria.

"Well, stop playing games and get to work," her mother said. "And have a nice dinner at Vickie's."

"Okay," said Maria, and hung up.

She was supposed to be at Vickie's? Vickie had invited Dr. Morthouse over and Dr. Morthouse had accepted?

It didn't make sense.

Puzzling over this, Maria turned toward the stairs. At the foot, she stopped. The staircase was steep. With a candle in one hand, she might lose her balance. Might fall and set the whole house on fire.

Dr. Morthouse really would kill her.

Maria put her foot on the first stair and bent over to take off her blades.

Something leaped out and grabbed her. "Aha!" a voice cried.

"Aaaaaaaaaahhhhrrr!" Maria was screaming more loudly than she'd ever screamed in her life. She threw the candle in the air. It turned end over end and went out, trailing a streamer of ghost-gray smoke as it fell to the floor.

Small, determined hands closed around her jacket.

Maria tore free and raced up the stairs into the dark.

*   *   *

The second bedroom to the left at the top of the stairs looked like no bedroom Vickie had ever seen.

For one thing, she couldn't find a bed. This was going to make hiding more difficult. Maybe, she thought, she could hide in that big mahogany wardrobe against the far wall. She tiptoed over and tried the handle.

It was locked.

This was not good.

That's what I get for listening to Maria, thought Vickie disgustedly. She tiptoed quickly out of the room and into the hall. One after the other she tried all the other doors in the hall.

All the other rooms were completely empty.

She'd almost reached the end of the hall and the last door, a much larger, heavier door than the rest, when she heard the scream.

"Maria!" she gasped, and turned too quickly.

The candle flame stretched out into a thin line and the darkness closed down around her.

Maria didn't know how she got up the stairs, but she did, blades and all. She couldn't hear Dr. Morthouse behind her. She was breathing too hard and her heart was pounding too loudly.

But when she reached the top of the stairs and paused, Dr. Morthouse was right behind her. A hand brushed her ankle.

"I'm gonna get you," snarled Dr. Morthouse.

Maria fled into the darkness. She crashed against a door and it flew open.

Dr. Morthouse paused and smiled in the darkness. "You've had it now, Maria," she said.

The light of a candle that had almost gone out and had then leaped to life again blazed in front of Dr. Morthouse's face. Lit up her diabolical smile.

Vickie stood there, her face pale, her eyes enormous.

"M-Maria? Did you get your skates—"

Dr. Morthouse—in Maria's body—smiled another evil smile.

Vickie leaped back. "You're not Maria!" she cried.

"Surprise, surprise!" howled Dr. Morthouse. She made a grab for the candle, but Vickie twisted away.

"Stay away from me!" Vickie shouted. "Heeeelp. Heeeelllllp!"

Dr. Morthouse sprang again.

Still managing to keep the candle burning, Vickie fled down the hall. She knew the rooms were empty. She knew that to dash into one of them was to dash into a trap. She made for the only door she hadn't tried.

The door at the end of the hall.

Crouched inside the dark room, Maria—in Dr. Morthouse's body—tried to make herself think calmly. *You're bigger than she is,* she told herself.

But she's meaner than you, her self answered.

You can outrun her.

But not in the dark.

You—

From the other side of the door, a familiar voice said, "Maria? Did you get your skates—"

Vickie! What was Vickie doing here?

Before she could figure it out, Vickie screamed a bloodcurdling scream.

Maria leaped to the door and flung it open.

A horrible sight met her eyes. By the wavering light of a candle, she saw Vickie Wheilson running away down the hall. Dr. Morthouse (in Maria's body), hands outstretched like claws, was one step behind.

Vickie lunged for the door at the end of the hall.

Dr. Morthouse lunged for Vickie.

"Dr. Morthouse! No!" screamed Maria, before she could stop herself.

Vickie froze. Dr. Morthouse froze. Then, slowly, she turned.

"Maria?" Dr. Morthouse asked in a soft, friendly voice that made Maria's blood run cold. "Maria, is that you?"

Vickie's pale face grew even paler. Her mouth dropped open with shock as she looked from one to the other.

"Yes," answered Maria. To her amazement, her voice wasn't trembling.

I'm bigger than she is, I'm bigger than she is, I'm

bigger than she is . . . She forced herself to walk slowly toward the two of them. She cleared her throat.

Dr. Morthouse's eyebrows snapped together in a ferocious frown.

"Quit frowning," said Maria. "You're giving me wrinkles." She stopped, well out of Dr. Morthouse's reach.

Vickie said, "Maria? *Maria?* You look . . . awful!"

Dr. Morthouse snapped, "Watch your language, young lady." Then she turned to Maria. "This is all your fault! You'll be sorry for this!"

"But I didn't do it! I don't know how it happened!" said Maria. "I hate it!" She grabbed at the collar of her blouse and gave it a yank. It ripped.

"Stop that! That's my good blouse!" Dr. Morthouse doubled up her fists.

And suddenly Maria knew that Dr. Morthouse couldn't hurt her. Because anything she did to Maria, she did to herself.

Maria reached up and gave the pearls a yank, too. They broke and slid to the ground.

Dr. Morthouse said, "You'll be sorry for this."

"What're you going to do?" Maria taunted.

Dr. Morthouse raised her hands. Maria held up one of hers. "I wouldn't if I were you, Doc. You want your body returned in the condition in which you left it, don't you? Undamaged? No bones broken? Like that?"

Slowly Dr. Morthouse lowered her hands. She glared at Maria.

Behind her, Vickie whispered, "April Fools' Day," in a dazed sort of way.

"I wish," said Maria.

"It *is* you," said Vickie.

"Yeah."

"But how long . . . ?"

"Since we collided in the hall this morning. One minute I was me and the next minute . . ." Maria shuddered.

"But this is excellent," said Vickie. "You can rule the world. Have Graveyard School torn down. Hire the pizza parlor to make lunch for us *every* day!"

Maria rolled her eyes.

Dr. Morthouse said, "I don't think so." She turned to glare at Vickie over her shoulder, and Vickie seemed to regain her senses. She shrank back.

"I just want to be me again," said Maria.

She and Dr. Morthouse stared at each other by the flickering light of the candle.

Stupid to have ever wished to be Dr. Morthouse. It wasn't fun, it was awful. What was she going to do?

Somewhere, far away, a clock began to chime.

"Midnight?" said Vickie in a puzzled voice.

"Always," said Dr. Morthouse proudly.

"I wish I were myself again," whispered Maria.

Vickie said, "I gotta get out of here!"

She broke past Dr. Morthouse, past Maria, and headed for the stairs.

"Oh no you don't!" shouted the principal. She leaped forward, her hands back in their raptor position, her eyes blazing fire.

Maria's nerve broke. She turned and ran, too.

She never knew what happened next. One minute she was running after the guttering light of the candle still clutched in Vickie's hand.

The next minute she was falling, head over heels, down the thickly carpeted stairs. She crashed into Vickie. She felt something crash into her from behind.

Down, down, down they went. They landed in a heap on the floor.

The candle blew out and everything went dark.

CHAPTER
11

Maria opened her eyes.

It was very, very dark. Very, very still.

She tried to remember where she was. Her head ached.

Someone, or something, was lying across her legs. The cat? She pushed.

It rolled sideways and groaned.

Something else groaned, too, in the darkness nearby.

She wasn't in her own bed. It wasn't the cat.

And then it all came back to her.

"No!" she cried, and shot upright.

She scrambled to her feet.

A hand curled around her ankle. She kicked out.

"Owww! Wait a minute! It's me!"

"Vickie?"

"We gotta get out of here."

"Where's here? It's totally dark."

"The candle . . . the table is next to the stairs. If you—"

"Gotcha."

In the nearby darkness, Dr. Morthouse groaned again.

Keeping one hand on the banister, Maria slid along the hall until she bumped into something. She put one hand down and touched something cold and hard.

The candles. Quickly she found the matches and lit one. Holding it high, she turned and went back down the hall.

Vickie was sitting upright on the floor, rubbing her forehead. "Good thing that carpet is thick," she said. "But did both of you have to land on me?"

"Could we not talk interior decoration here?" said Maria. "We've got to get out of here before Dr. Morthouse comes to."

But it was already too late. Dr. Morthouse's eyes opened. They stared up into nothing for a second.

Then she sat up with horrifying suddenness.

She smiled. Something silver glinted in her mouth.

That was when Maria realized that the best had happened.

Somehow, in the fall, she and Dr. Morthouse had switched places. She was herself again, Maria Medina in Maria Medina's body.

"It's me! Vickie, it's me! Check it out!"

"I know it's you!" cried Vickie. "Look at that smile!"

Dr. Morthouse smiled more widely than ever.

She got to her knees. Holding on to the banister, she pulled herself to her feet.

"Very funny, Ms. Medina," she said. "I suppose this was your idea of an April Fools' joke. Well, I've got a little joke for you—"

"Run!" screamed Vickie. "Run for your life!"

She and Maria ran toward the massive front door. They jerked it open. It screamed on its hinges.

But not as loudly as they were screaming.

Behind them, Dr. Morthouse leaped forward, too.

But she missed. She threw her hands out and flailed wildly. Her legs went into a bone-crunching split. Then her feet flew out from under her.

She landed with a house-shaking thud, the blades on her feet spinning in the air.

Vickie grabbed her board and she and Maria raced down the dark driveway into the street. Far, far away, a single streetlamp had flickered on.

"Wait!" cried Maria. "How do I know it's you? What if you and Dr. Morthouse switched places? What if this is a trick?"

Vickie managed to grin. "Can Dr. Morthouse board? I think not." She dropped the board and put one foot on it. "Hop on," she said. "We've got a long way to go."

It wasn't as late as they'd thought. It was midnight only in Dr. Morthouse's house. Maria and Vickie took turns pushing the board along and giving each other rides through the narrow twisted streets.

"This is the weirdest neighborhood I've ever been in," said Vickie.

"Outside of the graveyard, you mean," answered Maria. "Can you believe all this?"

"April Fools' Day," said Vickie. "To the max."

"What do you think made it happen?"

Vickie didn't answer right away. The streets were looking more normal now. They went down a hill and suddenly everything looked familiar. Safe.

A few minutes later they'd reached Maria's house. Maria got off the board.

"I don't know how it happened," said Vickie suddenly. "But you know it had to have something to do with the graveyard."

She pushed off and disappeared into the night.

Maria went into the house. The graveyard. She remembered talking about what it would be like to be Dr. Morthouse up there. But how had it all come true? And why?

"Maria, is that you?" said her mother's voice from the den.

Maria looked in. Her mother and father were watching television.

"You're home early, dear," said her mother. "Is everything all right?"

"These and other unsolved mysteries have haunted human beings since the dawn of time," an announcer intoned from the television.

"Good show," her father said. " 'The World of the Weird.' Want to watch with us?"

"No," said Maria firmly. "No thanks. It's a little too weird for me."

She had to go into the school sometime. If she skipped classes, her mother and father would find out and she'd be grounded until she was thirty.

Maria took a deep breath.

The other students had gone in. Maria and Vickie were still hovering outside, on the lower steps, in first-grade land.

But even the first-graders had left their stairs to go to school.

"She's in there," said Maria. "I can feel her. Waiting for us."

"What's she gonna do?" Vickie asked for maybe the hundredth time.

"I don't want to think about it."

"You're right."

Maria took a deep breath. "Let's run for it," she said.

They ran.

Iron hands fell on Vickie's left shoulder and Maria's right shoulder as they crossed the threshold of the school.

"Well, well, well," said Dr. Morthouse.

"Aaaaaahhh!" screamed Vickie.

"Arrrrrwww!" screamed Maria.

Heads turned. People stopped to stare.

Dr. Morthouse smiled.

Everyone started moving again, pretending they'd seen nothing at all.

Cowards, thought Maria disgustedly, trying in vain to twist free.

But she knew from *very* personal experience that Dr. Morthouse was too strong.

They stopped struggling. They hung limp as fish on a hook, awaiting their fates.

Dr. Morthouse leaned forward. "Don't ever let that happen again, do you understand?"

They both nodded.

The principal straightened up. She let them go. "Have a nice day," she said.

They ran.

"And don't run!" she ordered, and howled with evil laughter.

Stacey skated back up the hill and sat down. "You're lucky you didn't get in more trouble for skating in the hall," she said.

"Uh-huh," said Skate. He dropped his board and took off.

Skate, Vickie, Stacey, and Maria were up on Skateboard Hill. Maria was wearing her old blades.

"But I still don't think she should be allowed to just keep your blades."

Maria shrugged. It wasn't something she really wanted to talk about.

"I think you should go demand that she give them back."

Vickie snorted. "Yeah. Right."

"Well, maybe your mother could, then."

"I'll think about it," said Maria. And she would. But she wouldn't do anything about it.

Let Dr. Morthouse keep the skates. It was a small price to pay to have escaped April Fools' Day alive.

"We have time for one more run," said Stacey. She tightened one boot.

"Don't you wish—" Vickie began. A cold wind spun up out of nowhere and brushed past them with a faintly mocking sound.

"No wishes," said Maria, and took off. Stacey and Maria followed.

They wheeled down the long, long hill, carefully turning aside where the road forked and led into the graveyard.

The sun was almost out of sight as they reached the bottom.

Skate was standing there, board tucked up under one arm. But he wasn't watching them.

He was staring past them, a frown on his face.

"What is it?" asked Vickie quickly. "A skeleton? On a skateboard?"

"What are you talking about?" demanded Maria.

Skate shook his head. "Nothing." He gave Vickie a warning look.

Then he said, "It's kind of weird, though. I was sure I saw someone else up there—on blades. An adult . . ."

"No way," said Stacey.

"Yeah," said Vickie. "No way."

"Let's get home," said Maria quickly.

They turned to go.

But Maria looked back. She frowned. It wasn't possible. Was it?

Nah.

April Fools', she thought, and headed home.

CHAPTER
12

High above the old graveyard, up on Skateboard Hill, a skeleton on a skateboard swept into view. It hung an impossible flip and then landed without a sound. Sparks flew from the wheels of its board as it sped down the hill and onto the road that led through the graveyard and the treacherous stretch of pavement known as Dead Man's Curve.

Another figure emerged.

Its arms flailed wildly. It wasn't exactly steady on its feet. But sparks flew from the shining new set of blades strapped to its feet.

"Wait for me," it shouted. "Wait for meeeeeeee!"

And disappeared into the graveyard.

Here are a few April Fools' jokes to play on your friends:

1. Take a sandwich cookie, open it, and carefully scrape off the white filling. Replace the filling with toothpaste. Serve it up—and laugh!

2. Call a friend (with a good sense of humor) the night before April Fools' Day. Tell your friend that the whole class is planning to wear all their clothes backward for the occasion. Wait till you see that friend's face the next day—when he or she is the only one with clothes on backward!

3. Change the book covers on a friend's books when he or she isn't looking. When it's time for math, your friend will pull out an English book or vice versa!

Happy April Fools' Day
from
Tom B. Stone!